Dedicated to:

Spiritual masters, Sri Aurobindo and The Mother; My parents who have always been friends, philosophers, and guides to me; Shital, my loving husband and Param's father; My brother, aunts, uncles, parents-in-law; All who have touched our lives with love, kindness, and friendship.

Thanks to Katrina, Kalpana, Falguni, Maria, Nirmal, Pavithra, Pinky, Snigdha, Sangeetha, Shilpi, Shubhangi, Saif, Deepa, Vivek Kansara, and all friends and family for their feedback and contribution to this project.

Special thanks to dear friends Ashesh Joshi, Auroville, and Jeff Weinberg

www.mascotbooks.com

We Are One

©2017 Pinky Mukhi. All Rights Reserved. No part of this publication may be reproduced, stored in a retrieval system or transmitted in any form by any means electronic, mechanical, or photocopying, recording or otherwise without the permission of the author.

For more information, please contact:
Mascot Books
560 Herndon Parkway #120
Herndon, VA 20170
info@mascotbooks.com

Library of Congress Control Number: 2016920969

CPSIA Code: PRT0717A
ISBN-13: 978-1-63177-847-6

Printed in the United States

WE ARE ONE

Concept by Param Patel & Pinky Mukhi

Illustrated by Devika Joglekar

MINTU-

"I am very curious and observant. Nothing misses my eyes! I like to do things my way. I want to be a soccer player."

CHIRPY-

"I love learning new words and talking a lot. I am fascinated with the planets, stars, and galaxies, so I want to be an astronaut when I grow up."

CURIO-

"I love to explore everything! I have lots of energy and bang around the house, so my mom calls me a firecracker. I want to be an explorer."

"Mom," Mintu said. "I don't think I want to have my friends over for dinner tonight anymore."

"What?" Mintu's mother looked up from her cooking. "Why not, Mintu? It's almost dinnertime, and they will be here soon. Is something wrong?" She asked him in Gujarati, the Indian language they spoke at home.

"Mom, let's only speak English when my friends get here, okay?"

Mintu's mother was making paratha, a bread that was one of his favorite foods. But he was worried that his friends would find it strange. He had never seen paratha in anyone else's lunchbox at school. It smelled, looked, and tasted different from the foods he saw his friends eat. He was worried his friends would find him strange for liking it.

"Don't worry," his mother assured him. "Your friends love you for who you are, not what kinds of food you eat or what language you speak, silly! And besides, it's fun to try new things."

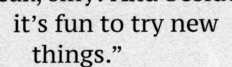

Mintu thought the paratha smelled delicious, and he wondered if his friends would agree. He hoped his friends liked the spiced vegetables they would wrap up in the tasty bread.

He knew his friends liked to play soccer and tag. He knew they all loved to learn and laugh at school together. But Mintu didn't know if they liked Indian food. Would they make fun of him if they didn't?

When the doorbell rang, Mintu had butterflies in his stomach. He took a deep breath and opened the door.

"Hi Curio! Hi Chirpy!" he said. "Come in!"

Right away, Curio noticed the aroma

coming from the kitchen. "Is your mom cooking?" he asked. "Her food smells so yummy! It makes me feel hungry like a bear."

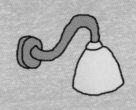

"My food is so different," Mintu said shyly.

"That's okay," Chirpy told Mintu. "I like trying new foods!"

"My food is different too," Curio said. "My family is from Mexico. My mom cooks Mexican food."

Mintu felt a little better. He was grateful that his friends were so nice. He decided he was glad his friends came over to dinner after all.

"Kids!" Mintu's mother called. "The paratha is done. Dinner is ready!"

At dinner, Chirpy asked, "Is paratha an English word?"

Mintu explained that paratha was an Indian word. He told them that he spoke an Indian language with his family.

"I speak another language too!" Curio said. "My family speaks Spanish at home."

Chirpy said, "Wow! I wish I spoke another language. I know my grandma can speak Italian."

As they ate their dinner, Curio said that the paratha reminded him of a tortilla. "Tortilla is a Spanish word," he said.

"I eat tortillas at home all the time," Chirpy said. "I've got to tell my mom to make paratha also!"

Mintu felt so happy that his friends liked Indian food! *I guess they don't find me strange after all*, he thought.

"I finished all my dinner. I am going to be taller and stronger. I wish I could be taller than a giraffe so I could reach treetops and eat fruits from trees," Mintu announced proudly.

Curio joined
in, "I'm smaller than you, but
I wish I could be tinier than
an elf so I could hide when I'm
naughty and no one would
find me." Curio let out a
mischievous laugh.

Chirpy said, "I'm medium-
sized. I like the way I am, but I
wish I had a very light body so I could
go to space and explore!"

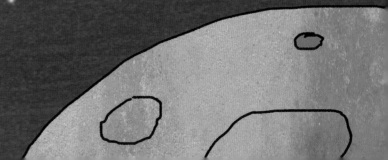

"We are not only different sizes. We even have different skin and hair colors," Mintu then realized.

"You are right. My skin color is different than yours!" Curio agreed.

"I wish I had blue skin and orange hair, my favorite colors," Mintu imagined.

"I would love to have pink skin and purple hair," Chirpy said excitedly.

Curio said with wide eyes, "Blue skin? Purple hair? You would look like butterflies! We have finished dinner, can we go play now?"

Mintu, Curio, and Chirpy giggled and walked like butterflies to the playroom.

Curio laughed and said, "We are going bananas!"

In the playroom, Mintu took out his favorite board game and asked the others if they would play with him.

Chirpy said, "Mintu, why don't you help me with this planet puzzle?"

Curio was engrossed. "Maybe later. I am experimenting with your magnets."

Mintu was disappointed when they said no to playing the game. "I want to play with you, but you won't. You are not my friends!" he frowned and stomped out of the room.

Mintu started crying as he went to find his mom. "They won't play with me! They are not my friends!" he wailed.

Mintu's mom brought him back to the playroom, comforting him. "Mintu, your friends are excited to play with your toys right now. Everybody has different likes and dislikes, but they are still your friends."

"I'm still mad!" Mintu said. "I want to play my game!"

Mintu's mom put her hand on his shoulder and told him "We all get mad sometimes."

"We all get sad sometimes, too. I feel sad that you're saying we're not your friends," Chirpy added.

"We also feel happy sometimes. I'll feel happy if you smile, Mintu!" Curio said.

Reluctantly, Mintu started to smile a little bit. Chirpy and Curio cheered, glad to see their friend smiling again.

Mintu was still confused. "Mom, we're all so different! We all eat different food, speak different languages, have different skin and hair colors, and even like to play different games! How are we still friends?"

Mintu's mom explained, "Your differences make you special and unique. It means that there's no one else like you. But we all feel similar emotions, like love. Love is something deep inside us."

"I think love comes from our heart. So I can't touch it like I can touch my head," Curio said.

"We can't see it, but we can feel it when we care about others and they care about us," Chirpy replied.

"I feel love when I help others," said Mintu. "And when I pray at night."

Mintu's mom agreed, "That's right! No matter what food you eat or what language you speak, love brings us closer and connects us all."

Suddenly, Mintu was feeling sad and embarrassed. He dropped his head and said, "I'm sorry I said that you weren't my friends. It's okay that we're all different. I love you all, and you love me too! We are one in love."

"Yes, we love you. We are one in love," all the kids agreed. They all hugged each other, forming a circle.

Even though they were different, the children felt closer than ever. They laughed as they went back to exploring their own interests. Mintu helped Chirpy with the puzzle and experimented with magnets with Curio.

They even had time to play Mintu's game together. Mintu felt he was the luckiest kid in the world to have such great friends.

Soon it was time for
Mintu's friends to go home.

"Thank you for sharing your
dinner with us," Curio said.
"Next week, you should come
over to my house for dinner!"

"I would love to taste your mom's Mexican food," Mintu smiled.

"Me too!" said Chirpy.

"Goodbye," said Chirpy.

"Adios," said Curio.

"Aavjo—visit me again," said Mintu.

We are brown.

We are **black**.

We are white.

We are colorful.

We come in different siZes.

We come in different shapes.

We speak different languages.

We celebrate different festivals.

We eat different food.

We like different things.

We are so different.

We are friends.

We help each other.

We feel sad for others.

We love each other.

Love is something deep in us.

We feel one with all we love.

We are one in love.

PARATHA RECIPE

PARATHA is flat unleavened bread made with or without spices. It can be made mixed with or stuffed with spices, vegetables, lentils, cheese, or paneer to make it more nutritious and delicious.

INGREDIENTS

2 cups of wheat flour
1 tsp oil/butter
1/2 tsp salt or as per taste
Water as needed

INSTRUCTIONS

1. Take a mixing bowl. Add 2 cups of flour.
2. Add salt and oil/butter and mix it well with the flour.
3. Knead the dough with water. Make a soft dough.
4. Take little dough to make a ball.
5. Roll the dough to make it round. Use some dry flour to help with rolling.
6. Heat the griddle and cook the paratha on one side.
7. Take some oil in a spoon and spread on the edge of the paratha on griddle.
8. Flip the paratha and cook the other side. Then the paratha is ready!